To
Ian

SIXTY-MINUTE SHAKESPEARE

HAMLET

by
Cass Foster

First Edition 1990.
Second Edition 1997.Third Edition 1998.Fourth Edition 2000.
All rights reserved. Printed in the United States of America.

Library of Congress Cataloging-in-Publication Data

Foster, Cass, 1948—
   The Sixty-Minute Shakespeare--[abridged] / Cass Foster.--1st ed.
      p. Cm. —(Classics for all ages)
   Summary: An abridged version of Shakespeare's tragedy about a young prince driven to avenge his father's murder.

ISBN: 1-877749-40-0

1. Princes—Denmark—Juvenile drama. 2. Children's plays,
English. [1. Plays.] I. Shakespeare, William. 1564-1616.
Hamlet. II. Title. III. Series.
PR2807.A25 1997
822.3'3—dc21   97-28920
                                                CIP
                                                AC

Cover Design by Barbara Kordesh
Paul M. Howey, Copy Editor

© 1990, 1997, 1998 and 2000 by Cass Foster

Five Star Publications, Incorporated
P.O. Box 6698
Chandler, AZ 85246-6698
websiter: www.fivestarsupport.com
e-mail: info@fivestarsupport.com

Five Star Publications, Incorporated

Where education comes naturally.

The Sixty-Minute Shakespeare:

Hamlet

by
Cass Foster

from

The Tragedy of Hamlet, Prince of Denmark

by
William Shakespeare

Five Star Publications, Incorporated ★ Chandler, AZ

Welcome to *The Sixty-Minute Shakespeare*

Thanks to the progressive thinking of so many curriculum developers, Language Arts people and the splendid film work being done by directors such as Kenneth Branagh and Franco Zeffirelli, there has been a phenomenal growth in interest in Shakespeare.

No playwright, past or present, approaches the brilliance and magnitude of William Shakespeare. What other individual has even come close to understanding and then dramatizing the human condition? Just for the fun of it, I am listing (following these introductory remarks) a sample of themes and images so richly developed in the canon of his plays.

Shakespeare's characters are so well-rounded and beautifully constructed that it is common to see them as actual historical figures. When someone mentions Hamlet, Iago, Ophelia, or Puck, we immediately experience images and emotions that come from memories of people we know. We may feel compassion, frustration, sorrow, or pleasure.

As one of the wealthiest people of his times, Shakespeare earned his living as a playwright, theatre manager, actor, and shareholder in the Globe Theatre. He worked tirelessly to entertain. (Theatres presented a new play every day and the average new play had a total of only ten performances over an entire season.) He rebelled against the contemporary theatrical standards (the neo-classical principles that limited dramatic structure throughout France and Italy), he took plots from other published works (making them uniquely his own), and he created a spectacle (without the use of elaborate scenery) to captivate audiences of all social levels.

Imagine the challenge in quieting a crowd of three thousand in a theatre where vendors sell wine, beer, ale, nuts, and cards; where there is no intermission; where birds fly overhead; and where audience members stand near performers. Such was the settings which Shakespeare's plays were originally staged.

The world's most familiar and successful wordsmith used language to skillfully create images, plot, and a sense of music and rhythm. The purpose behind this series is to reduce (not contemporize) the language. The unabridged Shakespeare simply isn't practical in all situations. Not all educators or directors have the luxury of time to explore the entire text. This is not intended to be a substitute for a thorough study of Shakespeare. It is merely a stepping stone.

I challenge each of you to go beyond the *Sixty-Minute* versions. Use the comfort, appreciation, and self-confidence you will gain to go further. Be proud of the insights and knowledge you acquire but do not be satisfied. The more you read, the more you gain.

I would love to know what you like about the design of this series and what we might do to improve it. I encourage our readers outside the United States to let me know how well this series works for you. It would also help to know what other Shakespearean plays you would like in the *Sixty-Minute* format. **Please e-mail me at** *casspeare@usa.net.*

May each of you be blessed with an abundance of good health and happiness. I thank you for your interest in our work and hope your are pleased with what we have done.

May the Verse Be With You!

A couple of staging considerations.

Scenery

There are two excellent reasons theatres rarely use much scenery when staging Shakespeare. The first is related to the number of changes required. If we have to wait every five to ten minutes to watch scenery struck and set up, we end up watching a play about moving lumber. The second reason is that we lose sight of what the play is about. Audiences need a couple minutes to adjust to the new scenic look of a dazzling waterfall and lush forest. By the time they take it all in and start paying attention to what the actors are saying, it is time to set up the next scene and the audience is lost.

Location is normally established through dialogue and the use of a few simple props: a throne-like chair for the king's court, a long table with benches for an inn, or a bed for the queen's bed chamber. The key is to keep it simple.

Pacing

You will want to keep things moving all the time. That doesn't mean actors should talk and move quickly; it simply means one scene should flow smoothly to the next without delay or interruption.

As scene one ends, the actors pick up their props and walk off. Actors for scene two enter from a different direction with their props and begin dialogue as soon as they enter the acting area, putting their props in place as they speak. Yes, we will still have view of the actors in the first scene, but your audience will gladly accept this convention if it means taking fifteen minutes off performance time.

v

Looking for additional suggestions in staging plays?

Check with Five Star Publications, Incorporated for the release date of

The Director's Companion
by
Cass Foster

This unique "how-to" in directing is geared for directors in elementary and secondary education. This practical, easy-to-read guide is designed to assist directors working with all styles of theatre. Whether classical, contemporary, comedy, tragedy, musicals, or theatre-for-youth, it's all there. Consider this constant and friendly companion your mentor as it helps you to simplify your work and increase creative contributions from everyone involved. Look for valuable insights in working with

Boredom
Discipline
Writing Plays
Improvisation
Script Analysis
Directing Styles
Body and Voice
Musical Theatre
Iambic Pentameter
Audience Etiquette
Planning Rehearsals
Working with Comedy
How to Write a Critique
Director Responsibilities
Role of the Stage Manager
Actor/Director Relationship
Interdisciplinary Opportunities
Communicating with Designers
Memorization and Concentration
Staging Fights and Crowd Scenes
Auditions and Non-Traditional Casting
Involving Colleagues and Administrators

Be sure to order a copy for home and the classroom.

Images and themes to look for in the various plays

Mistaken identity
Insanity
Religious persecution
The supernatural
Loneliness or isolation
Conspiracy
Hypocrisy
Pride
Violence
Rebellion
Seduction
Loyalty
Marriage
Irresponsible power
Real or pretended madness
Tyranny
Spying
Play-acting
Heavenly retribution
Witchcraft
Self-destruction
Animals
Reality vs. illusion
Characters reforming
Freedom
Fertility
Sexual misadventure
Corrupt society
Multiple meanings of words
Impetuous love
Human frailty
Charity

Wisdom of fools
Greed and corruption
The elements
Darkness and light
Anti-Semitism
Revenge
Abandonment
Honor
Bravery
Savagery
Disease or physical decay
War
False accusations
Destiny or fate
Ambition
Foils or opposites
Paranoia
Justice
Forgiveness
Mortality
Black or white magic
Nature
Astrological influence
Old age
Usurping of power
Suppression
Melancholy
Love and/or friendship
Thought vs. action
Role of women
Preparing for leadership
Betrayal

The Complete Works of William Shakespeare

1589 - 1591	Henry VI, Part 1, 2 and 3
1592 - 1593	Richard III
1593 - 1594	Titus Andronicus
1592 - 1594	Comedy of Errors
1593 - 1594	Taming of the Shrew
1594	The Two Gentlemen of Verona
1594 - 1595	Love's Labour's Lost
1594 - 1596	King John
1595	Richard II
1595 - 1596	A Midsummer Night's Dream
1595 - 1596	Romeo and Juliet
1596 - 1597	The Merchant of Venice
1597	The Merry Wives of Windsor
1597 - 1598	Henry IV, Part 1 and 2
1598 - 1599	Much Ado About Nothing
1599	Henry V
1599	Julius Caesar
1599	As You Like It
1600 - 1601	Hamlet
1601 - 1602	Twelfth Night
1601 - 1602	Troilus and Cressida
1602 - 1603	All's Well That Ends Well
1604	Measure for Measure
1604	Othello
1605	The Tragedy of King Lear
1606	Macbeth
1606 - 1607	Antony and Cleopatra
1607 - 1608	Timon of Athens
1607 - 1608	Pericles, Prince of Tyre
1607 - 1608	Coriolanus
1609 - 1610	Cymbeline
1609 - 1610	The Winter's Tale
1611	The Tempest
1612 - 1613	Henry VIII
1613	Two Noble Kinsmen (Authorship in question.)

April 23, 1564 - April 23, 1616

"If we wish to know the force of human genius, we should read Shakespeare. If we wish to see the insignificance of human learning, we may study his commentators."

William Hazlitt (1778-1830), English Essayist. "On the Ignorance of the Learned," in *Edinburgh Magazine* (July, 1818).

Common Quotes from the Bard.

Romeo and Juliet

> Parting is such sweet sorrow.
> A plague o' both your houses.
> O Romeo, Romeo! Wherefore art thou Romeo?

A Midsummer Night's Dream

> Lord, what fools these mortals be.
> The course of true love never did run smooth.
> To say the truth, reason and love keep little company
> together now-a-days.

As You Like It

> All that glisters is not gold.
> Love is blind.
> All the world's a stage
> And all the men and women merely players.
> For ever and a day.

Twelfth Night

> Some are born great, some achieve greatness, and some have
> greatness thrust upon them.
> Out of the jaws of death.
> O, had I but followed the arts!
> Many a good hanging prevents a bad marriage.

Henry IV, Part 1

> The better part of valour is discretion.
> To give the devil his due.
> He hath eaten me out of house and home.

King Lear

> The Prince of Darkness is a gentleman.

Henry VI, Part 2

> Let's kill all the lawyers.

The Merry Wives of Windsor

> Better three hours too soon than a minute too late.

Common Quotes from the Bard.

Macbeth

> Out, damned spot. Out, I say!
> Screw your courage to the sticking place.

Hamlet

> Something is rotten in the state of Denmark.
> To be or not to be. That is the question.
> The lady doth protest too much, methinks.
> Good night, sweet prince, And flights of angels
> sing thee to thy rest!

The Merchant of Venice

> The devil can cite scriptures for his purpose.

Pericles

> Few love to hear the sins they love to act.

Richard III

> Now is the winter of our discontent.
> Off with his head!
> A horse! A horse! My kingdom for a horse.

Julius Caesar

> Beware the ides of March.
> Friends, Romans, countrymen, lend me your ears.
> It was Greek to me.

Much Ado About Nothing

> The world must be peopled. When I said I would die a
> bachelor, I did not think I should live till I were
> married.

Measure for Measure

> The miserable have no other medicine but only hope.

Troilus and Cressida

> To fear the worst oft cures the worse.

The Comedy of Errors

> Unquiet meals make ill digestions.

Cast of characters

Ghost of Hamlet, the former King of Denmark.
Claudius, King of Denmark, former King's brother.
Gertrude, Queen of Denmark, widow of the former King
    and now wife of Claudius.
Hamlet, Prince of Denmark, son of the late King and of
    Gertrude.

Horatio, Hamlet's friend and fellow student.

Polonius, councillor to the King.
Laertes, his son.
Ophelia, his daughter.

Rosencrantz
Guildenstern   Members of the Danish Court.
Osric

Bernardo
Francisco   Officers and soldiers on watch.
Marcellus

Three players, player King, player Queen, and Lucianus.
A Gravedigger
Priest
Lords, soldiers, attendants, etc.

Place
Denmark

Act I, Scene 1.
The guard-platform of the castle.

Francisco standing guard. Enter Bernardo.

Bernardo. Who's there?

Francisco. Stand and unfold yourself!

Bernardo. Long live the king!

Francisco. Bernardo?

Bernardo. He.

Francisco. You come most carefully upon your hour.
Stand, ho! Who is there?

Horatio. Friends to this ground.

Marcellus. Holla! Bernardo!

Bernardo. Welcome Marcellus. Welcome, good Horatio.

Horatio. Has this thing appeared again tonight?

Francisco. I have seen nothing.

Marcellus. Horatio says 'tis but our fantasy.

Bernardo. Peace, break thee off! Look where it comes
again.

1

Francisco. It is the same figure like the King that's dead.

Marcellus. Thou art a scholar. Speak to it, Horatio.

Bernardo. Looks 'a not like the King? Mark it, Horatio.

Horatio. What art thou that usurp'st° this time of night,
    Together with that fair and warlike form
    In which the majesty of buried Denmark°
    Did sometime° march? By heaven, I charge thee speak!

Marcellus. See, it stalks away.

Horatio. Stay! Speak, speak! I charge thee, speak!

Ghost exits.

Francisco. 'Tis gone and will not answer.

Bernardo. How now, Horatio? You tremble and look pale.
    Is not this something more than fantasy?

Horatio. Before my G-d°, I might not this believe
    Without the sensible and true avouch°
    Of mine own eyes.

Marcellus.   Is it not like the King?

Usurp'st: wrongfully take over. *Buried Denmark:* buried King of Denmark.
Sometime: formerly. *G-d:* According to the editor's religious convictions, to
write out the name of the Supreme Being in full turns the text into a sacred
scripture. Out of respect for his beliefs, we will hyphenate all usage. *Avouch:*
evidence.

Horatio. As thou art to thyself.

Francisco. It faded on the crowing of the cock.

Horatio. Look, the morn in russet mantle clad
    Walks o'er the due of yon high eastward hill.
    Break we our watch up, and by my advice
    Let us impart what we have seen tonight
    Unto young Hamlet; for upon my life
    This spirit, dumb to us, will speak to him.

They exit.

Act I, Scene 2.

King enters with Gertrude, the Lords, Polonius, Laertes and Hamlet.

King. Though yet of Hamlet our dear brother's death
    The memory be green, and that it us befitted
    To bear our hearts in grief and our whole kingdom
    To be contracted in one brow of woe,
    Yet so far hath discretion fought with nature
    That we with wisest sorrow think on him
    Together with remembrance of ourselves.
    Therefore our sometime° sister, now our queen,
    Th' imperial jointress° to this warlike state,
    Have we, as 'twere with a defeated joy...
    With an auspicious and a dropping eye°,
    With mirth in funeral and with dirge in marriage,
    Taken to wife.

All but Hamlet applaud.

King. And now, Laertes, what's the news with you?
    What wouldst thou have, Laertes?

Laertes. My thoughts and wishes bend again toward
    France. And bow them to your gracious leave.

King. Have you your father's leave? What says Polonius?

Sometime: former.   *Jointress:* woman possessing property with her husband.
Auspicious and dropping eye: one eye smiling and the other weeping.

Polonius. H'ath, my lord, wrung from me my slow leave
    By laborsome petition, and at last
    Upon his will I sealed my hard consent.
    I do beseech you, give him leave to go.

King. Take thy fair hour, Laertes. Time be thine,
    And thy best graces spend it at thy will!°
    But now, my cousin Hamlet, and my son...

Hamlet. A little more than kin, and less than kind.°

King. How is it that the clouds still hang on you?

Hamlet. Not so, my lord. I am too much in the sun.°

Queen. Good Hamlet, cast thy nighted color° off,
    And let thine eye look like a friend on Denmark.
    Do not forever with thy failèd lids
    Seek for thy noble father in the dust.
    Thou know'st 'tis common, all that lives must die.

Hamlet. Ay, madam, it is common.

Queen.   If it be,
    Why seems it so particular with thee?

And...spend it at thy will: and my your best qualities guide you. *A little...kind:*
I am closer than a nephew (since you are my mother's husband) but, as a son, not
well disposed to you. *Sun:* Obvious pun on son. *Nighted color:* mourning
garments or dark melancholy.

Hamlet. Seems, madam? Nay, it is. I know not "seems."
    'Tis not alone my inky cloak, good mother,
    Together with all forms, moods, shades of grief,
    That can denote me truly. These indeed seem,
    For they are actions that a man might play.
    But I have that within which passes show;
    These but the trappings and the suits of woe.

King. 'Tis sweet and commendable in your nature, Hamlet
    To give these mourning duties to your father;
    But you must know your father lost a father,
    That father lost his. But to perserver
    In obstinate condolement° is a course
    Of impious stubbornness. 'Tis unmanly grief.
    It shows a will most incorrect to heaven.
                        For your intent
    In going back to school in Wittenberg,
    It is most retrograde to our desire.

Queen. Let not thy mother lose her prayers, Hamlet.
    I pray thee, stay with us, go not to Wittenberg.

Hamlet. I shall in all my best, obey you, madam.

King. Why, 'tis a loving and fair reply.
    Be as ourself in Denmark. Madam, come.
    This gentle and unforced accord of Hamlet
    Sits smiling to my heart.

All exit but Hamlet.

Condolement: grief.

Hamlet. O, that this too, too sullied° flesh would melt,
Thaw, and resolve itself into a dew!
Or that the Everlasting had not fixed
His cannon° 'gainst self-slaughter! O G-d, G-d,
How weary, stale, flat, and unprofitable
Seem to me all the uses of this world!
Fie on 't, ah fie! 'Tis an unweeded garden
That grows to seed. Things rank and gross in nature
Possess it merely. That it should come to this!
But two months dead...nay, not so much. Not two.
So excellent a king, that was to this
Hyperion° to a satyr°, so loving to my mother
That he might not beteem° the winds of heaven
Visit her face too roughly. Heaven and earth,
Must I remember? Why, she would hang on him
As if increase of appetite had grown
By what it fed on, and yet within a month...
Let me not think on 't; frailty, thy name is woman!

Enter Horatio, Marcellus and Bernardo.

Horatio. Hail to your lordship!

Hamlet.   I am glad to see you well.
Horatio! I am very glad to see you. *(To Bernardo.)*
Good even, sir...But what in faith make you from
Wittenberg? What is your affair in Elsinore?

Horatio. My lord, I came to see your father's funeral.

Sullied: defiled or solid.   *Cannon*: law.   *Hyperion*: sun-god.   *Satyr*: half-human mythical creature with goat's legs and horns.   *Beteem*: allow.

7

Hamlet. I prithee, do not mock me, fellow student;
    I think it was to see my mother's wedding.

Horatio. In deed, my lord, it followed hard upon.

Hamlet. Thrift, thrift, Horatio! The funeral baked meats
    Did coldly furnish forth the marriage tables.
    Would I had met my dearest foe in heaven
    Or ever I had seen that day, Horatio!
    My father! Methinks I see my father.

Horatio. Where, my lord?

Hamlet.   In my mind's eye, Horatio.

Horatio. My lord, I think I saw him yesternight.

Hamlet. Saw? Who?

Horatio. My lord, the King, your father.
    Two nights together had these gentlemen,
    Marcellus and Bernardo, on their watch,
    In the dead waste and middle of the night,
    Been thus encountered. A figure like your father.

Hamlet. But where was that?

Marcellus. My lord, upon the platform where we watch.

Hamlet. Did you not speak to it?

Horatio.   My lord, I did,
    But answer made it none.

Hamlet.   'Tis very strange.

Horatio. As I do live, my honored lord, 'tis true.

Hamlet. Indeed, indeed. But this troubles me.
    Hold you watch tonight?

All.   We do, my lord.

Hamlet. Than I too will watch tonight.
    Perchance 'twill walk again.

Horatio.   I warrant it.

Hamlet. If you have hitherto concealed this sight,
    Let it be tenable in your silence still.

All. Our duty to your honor.

Hamlet. Your loves, as mine to you. Farewell.

All but Hamlet exit.

Hamlet. My father's spirit in arms! All is not well.
    I doubt some foul play. Would the night were come!
    Till then, sit still, my soul. Foul deeds will rise,
    Though all the earth o'erwhelm them, to men's eyes.

Hamlet exits.

Act I, Scene 3.

The chamber of Polonius. Enter Laertes and Ophelia.

Laertes. My necessaries are embarked. Farewell.
    And for Hamlet, and the trifling of his favor;
    Hold it a fashion° and a toy in blood.

Ophelia. No more but so?

Laertes. Think it no more. But you must fear,
    His greatness weighed, his will is not his own.
    For he is the subject to his birth.
    He may not, as unvalued persons do,
    Carve for himself, for on his choice depends
    The safety and health of this whole state.

Enter Polonius.

Polonius. Yet here, Laertes? Aboard, aboard, for shame!
    The wind sits in the shoulder of your sail,
    And you are stayed for: There...my blessing with thee!
    And these few precepts in thy memory
    Look thou character°: Give thy thoughts no tongue,
    Nor any unproportioned° thought his act
    Be though familiar° but by no means vulgar°.
    Give every man thy ear, but few thy voice;
    Neither a borrower nor a lender be;
    For loan oft loses both itself and friend,
    And borrowing dulls the edge of husbandry°.

Fashion: standard behavior for a young man. *Look thou character:* be sure to
remember this. *Unproportioned;* badly calculated. *Familiar:* social. *Vulgar:*
common. *Husbandry:* thrift.

Polonius. This above all: to thine own self be true,
    And it must follow, as the night the day,
    Thou canst not then be false to any man.

Laertes. Most humbly do I take my leave, my lord.
    Farewell, Ophelia, and remember well
    What I have said to you.

Ophelia. 'Tis in my memory locked,
    And you yourself shall keep the key of it.

Laertes. Farewell.

Laertes exits.

Polonius. What is 't, Ophelia, he has said to you?

Ophelia. So please you, something touching the lord
    Hamlet.

Polonius. Marry°, well bethought.
    'Tis told me he hath very oft of late
    Given private time to you.

Ophelia. He hath, my lord, of late made many tenders°
    of his affection to me.

Polonius. Affection? Pooh!
    Do you believe his tenders, as you call them?

Marry: indeed. (originally the name of the Virgin Mary, used as an oath.)
Tenders: offers.

Ophelia. I do not know, my lord, what I should think.

Polonius. Marry, I will teach you.

Ophelia. My lord, he hath importuned me with love
   In honorable fashion.

Polonius. Ay, fashion you may call it. Go to, go to°.

Ophelia. And hath given countenance° to his speech, my
   lord, with all the holy vows of heaven.

Polonius. Ay, springes° to catch woodcocks°. I do know
   When the blood burns, how prodigal the soul
   Lends the tongue vows.
   I would not, in plain terms, from this time forth
   Have you so slander° any moment's leisure
   As to give words or talk with the Lord Hamlet.
   Look to 't, I charge you. Come your ways°.

Ophelia. I shall obey, my lord.

They exit.

Go to: expression of impatience. *Countenance:* authority. *Springes:* snares.
Woodcocks: gullible birds. *Slander:* abuse. *Come your ways*: come along.

Act I, Scene 4.

The guard-platform of the castle.

Enter Hamlet, Horatio and Marcellus.

Hamlet. The air bites shrewdly°; it is very cold.

Horatio. It is a nipping and eager air.

Hamlet. What hour now?

Horatio.　　　　　　　　　　I think it lacks of twelve.

Marcellus. No, it is struck.

Enter ghost.

Horatio. Look, my lord, it comes!

Hamlet. Angels and ministers of grace defend us!
　　Be thou a spirit of health or goblin damned,
　　Be thy intents wicked or charitable,
　　I will speak to thee. I'll call thee Hamlet,
　　King, father, royal Dane. O, answer me!

The ghost beckons Hamlet.

Hamlet. It will not speak. Then I will follow it.

Horatio. Do not, my lord!

Shrewdly: keenly.

13

Hamlet. Why, what should be the fear?
 I do not set my life at a pin's fee°,
 And for my soul, what can it do to that,
 Being a thing as immortal as itself?

Horatio. What if it tempt you toward the flood, my lord,
 Or the dreadful summit of the cliff
 And there assume some other horrible form
 Which might deprive your sovereignty of reason
 And draw you into madness

Hamlet. It wafts me still...Go on, I'll follow thee.

Marcellus. You shall not go, my lord.

They attempt to stop Hamlet.

Hamlet.   Hold off your hands!
 By heaven, I'll make a ghost of him that lets me!
 I say, away!...Go on, I'll follow thee.

Exit ghost and Hamlet.

Horatio. He waxes desperate with imagination.

Marcellus. Let's follow. 'Tis not fit thus to obey him.
 Something is rotten in the state of Denmark.

Horatio. Heaven will direct it°.

Marcellus. Nay, let's follow him. *(They exit.)*

Fee: value. *It*: the outcome.

14

Act I, Scene 5.

Ghost and Hamlet enter.

Ghost. I am thy father's spirit,
   Doomed for a certain term to walk the night,
   And for the day, confined to fast in fires.
                           But that I am forbid
   To tell the secrets of my prison house,
   I could a tale unfold whose lightest word
   Would harrow° up thy soul. List, list, O, list!
   If thou didst ever thy dear father love,
   Revenge his foul and most unnatural murder.

Hamlet. Murder?

Ghost. Murder most foul, as in the best it is,
   But this most foul, strange, and unnatural.

Hamlet. Haste me to know 't, that I, with wings as swift
   As meditation or the thoughts of love
   May sweep to my revenge.

Ghost. 'Tis given out that, sleeping in my orchard,
   A serpent stung me. But know, thou noble youth,
   The serpent that did sting thy father's life
   Now wears his crown.

Hamlet. O, my prophetic soul! My uncle!

Harrow: lacerate, tear.

Ghost. Ay, that incestuous, that adulterate beast,
    With witchcraft of his wit, with traitorous gifts
    won to his shameful lust
    The will of my most seeming-virtuous queen.
    But soft, methinks I scent the morning air.
    Brief let me be. Sleeping within my orchard,
    My custom always of the afternoon,
    Upon my secure hour thy uncle stole,
    With juice of cursèd hebona° in a vial,
    And in the porches of my ear did pour
    The leprous distillment.
    Thus was I, sleeping, by a brother's hand
    Cut off even in the blossoms of my sin,
    No reckoning° made, but sent to my account
    With all my imperfections on my head.
    Let not the royal bed of Denmark be
    A couch for luxury and damnèd incest.
    But, howsoever thou pursues this act,
    Taint not thy mind nor let thy soul contrive
    Against thy mother aught. Leave her to heaven...
                            Fare thee well at once.
    The glowworm shows the matin° to be near.
    Adieu, adieu, adieu! Remember me.

The ghost exits.

Hebona: poison.   *Reckoning*: settling of accounts or possible atonement.
Matin: morning.

Hamlet.   Remember thee?
   Ay, thou poor ghost, whiles memory holds a seat
   In this distracted globe°. Remember thee?
   Yea, from the table° of my memory
   I'll wipe away all trivial fond records.
   Thy commandments all alone shall live
   Within the book and volume of my brain,
   Unmixed with baser matter. Yes, by heaven!

He hears his uncle and mother laughing.

Hamlet. O most pernicious woman!
   O villain, villain, smiling, damnèd villain!
   My tables°...meet it is° I set it down
   That one may smile, and smile, and be a villain.
   So, uncle, there you are. Now to my word:
   It is "Adieu, adieu!" Remember me."
   I have sworn 't.

Enter Horatio and Marcellus.

Marcellus. How is 't, my noble lord?

Horatio. What news.

Hamlet. No, you will reveal it.

Horatio. Not I, my lord, by heaven.

Marcellus. Nor I, my lord.

Globe: head or world.   *Table:* slate.   *Tables:* writing tables.   *Meet it is:* it is fitting.

17

Hamlet. It is an honest ghost, that let me tell you...
   Give me one poor request.

Horatio. What is't, my lord? We will.

Hamlet. Never make known what you have seen tonight.

Horatio. In faith, my lord, not I.

Marcellus. Nor I, my lord, in faith.

Hamlet. Upon my word.

He holds out his sword.

Ghost. (From off stage.) Swear.

Hamlet. Come on, you hear this fellow in the cellarage.
   Consent to swear.

Horatio.   Propose the oath, my lord.

Hamlet. Never to speak of this that you have seen.
   Swear by my sword.

Ghost. (From off stage.) Swear.

*They take hold of the sword's hilt and swear. Hamlet
then moves to another spot.*

Hamlet. Swear by my sword
   Never to speak of this that you have heard.

Ghost. (From off stage.) Swear.

They swear on the sword and the ghost exits.

Hamlet. Rest, rest, perturbèd spirit.
   The time is out of joint. O cursèd spite
   That ever I was born to set it right!

Out of respect they indicate they will follow after him.

Hamlet. Nay, come, let's go together.

Act II, Scene 1.

The chamber of Polonius. Enter Polonius and Ophelia.

Polonius. How now, Ophelia, what's the matter?

Ophelia. O my lord, my lord, I have been so afrighted!

Polonius. With what, I' the name of G-d?

Ophelia. My lord, as I was sewing in my closet,
  Lord Hamlet, with his doublet all unbraced,
  No hat upon his head, his stockings fouled,
  Ungartered, and down-gyvèd° to his ankle,
  As if he had been loosed out of hell...
                              He comes before me.

Polonius. What said he?

Ophelia. He took me by the wrist and held me hard.
  He falls to such perusal of my face
  As 'a would draw it. Long stayed he so.
  And thrice his head thus waving up and down.
                        That done, he lets me go,
  And with his head over his shoulder turned
  He seemed to find his way without eyes.

Polonius.   I will go seek the King.
  This is the very ecstasy of love.
  Have you given him any hard words of late?

Down-gyvèd: fallen to the ankles.

Ophelia. No, my good lord, but as you did command
    I did repel his letters and denied his access to me.

Polonius. That hath made him mad.
    It is common for the younger sort to
    Lack discretion. Yea, I must to the King.

They exit.

Act II, Scene 2.

Enter the King, Queen, Rosencrantz and Guildenstern.

King. Welcome, dear Rosencrantz and Guildenstern.
                              I entreat you both
    That, being of so young days brought up with him,
    To draw him on to pleasures, and to gather
    So much as from occasion you may glean,
    Whether aught to us unknown afflicts him thus
    That opened, lies within our remedy.

Queen. Your visitation shall receive such thanks
    As fits a king's remembrance°.

Rosencrantz.   Both Your Majesties
    Might, by the sovereign power you have of us,
    Put your dread pleasures more into command
    Than to entreaty.

Guildenstern.   But we both obey,
    And here give up ourselves in the full bent
    To lay our service freely at your feet,
    To be commanded.

King. Thanks, Rosencrantz and gentle Guildenstern.

Queen. Thanks, Guildenstern and gentle Rosencrantz.
    And I beseech you instantly to visit
    My too much changèd son.

King's remembrance: a gift from a king who rewards his loyal subjects.

Rosencrantz and Guildenstern exit, awkwardly running into Polonius.

King. What news Polonius?

Polonius. (Catching his breath.) Your noble son is mad.
   That he is mad, 'tis true; 'tis true 'tis pity,
   And pity 'tis 'tis true.

Queen. More matter, with less art.

Polonius. Madam, I swear I use no art at all.
   Perpend.
   I have a daughter...have while she is mine...
   Who, in her duty and obedience, mark,
   Hath given me this. Now gather and surmise.
   (He reads the letter.) "To the celestial and my soul's
   idol, the most beautified Ophelia"...
   That's an ill phrase, a vile phrase; "beautified" is a vile
   phrase. *(King clears his throat.)* But you shall hear.

   (He reads.)   "Doubt° thou the stars are fire,
                        Doubt that the sun does move,
                          Doubt truth to be a liar,
                        But never doubt I love.
   Thine evermore, most dear lady, whilst this machine
   is to him, Hamlet."
   This in obedience hath my daughter shown me.

King. But how hath she received his love?

Doubt: suspect.

Polonius. What do you think of me?

King. As of a man faithful and honorable.

Polonius.   I would fain prove so...
    That she should lock herself from his resort°,
    And he, repellèd...a short tale to make...
    Fell into a sadness, then into a fast,
    Thence to a lightness°, and by this declension°
    Into the madness wherein now he raves
    And all we mourn for.

King. (To the queeen.) Do you think 'tis this?

Queen. It may be, very like.

Polonius. Take this from this°, if this be otherwise.

King. How may we try it further?

Polonius. You know sometimes he walks four hours
    together
    Here in the lobby.

Queen.   So he does indeed.

Polonius. At such a time I'll loose my daughter to him.

Resort: visits. *Lightness*: lightheadedness. *Declension*: deterioration. *Take this from this*: Polonius gestures cutting his throat, as if to cut off his head.

Polonius. (To the king.) Be you and I behind an arras°.
    Mark the encounter. If he love her not
    And be not from his reason fallen thereon,
    Let me be no assistant for a state.

Enter Hamlet, reading a book.

Queen. But look where sadly the poor wretch comes
    reading.

Polonius. I will board° him presently. Give me leave.

He gestures for the king and queen to quickly leave.

Polonius. How does my good lord, Hamlet?

Hamlet looks at him questionably.

Polonius. Do you know me, my lord?

Hamlet. Excellent well. You are a fishmonger°.

Polonius. Not I, my lord.

Hamlet. Than I would you were so honest a man.

Polonius. Honest, my lord?

Hamlet.   Have you a daughter?

Arras: hanging tapestry.   *Board*: accost.   *Fishmonger:* fish merchant.

Polonius. I have, my lord.

Hamlet. Let her not walk I' the sun. Conception is a
    blessing, but as your daughter may conceive, friend,
    look to 't. *(Hamlet continues reading.)*

Polonius. (Aside.)   Still harping on my daughter.
    What do you read, my lord?

Hamlet. Words, words, words.

Polonius. What is the matter°, my lord?

Hamlet. Between who?

Polonius. I mean the matter you read.

Hamlet. Slanders, sir; for the satirical rogue says here
    that old men have gray beards, that their faces are
    wrinkled, their eyes purging thick amber and plum-
    tree gum, and that they have a plentiful lack of wit.
    For yourself, sir, shall grow old as I am, if like a crab
    you could go backward.

Polonius. (Aside.) Though this be madness, yet there is
    method in 't. How pregnant sometimes his replies are!
    My honorable lord, I will most humbly take my leave
    of you.

Matter: subject of the book but Hamlet responds as if Polonius wants to know
"What is wrong?"   *Wit:* understanding.

Hamlet. You cannot, sir, take from me anything that I will
   more willingly part withal°...except my life, except my
   life, except my life.

Enter Rosencrantz and Guildenstern.

Polonius. Fare you well, my lord.

Hamlet. These tedious old fools!

Polonius. You go to seek the Lord Hamlet. There he is.

Rosencrantz. (To Polonius.) G-d save you, sir!

Polonius exits.

Guildenstern. My honored lord.

Rosencrantz. My most dear lord.

Hamlet. My excellent good friends! What make you at
   Elsinore?

Rosencrantz. To visit you, my lord. No other occasion.

Hamlet. Were you sent for? Is it a free visitation?...
   Come, come. Speak!

Guildenstern. What should we say, my lord?

Withal: with.

Hamlet. Anything but to the purpose. There is a kind of
   confession in your looks. I know the good King and
   Queen have sent for you.

Rosencrantz. To what end?

Hamlet. That you must teach me.

Guildenstern. My lord, we were sent for.

Hamlet. I will tell you why. I have of late...but wherefore
   I know not...lost all my mirth, forgone all custom of
   exercises; and indeed it goes so heavily with my
   disposition that this goodly frame, the earth, seems to
   me a sterile promontory; this most excellent canopy,
   the air, look you, this brave° o'erhanging firmament,
   this majestical roof fretted° with golden fire, why, it
   appeareth nothing to me but a foul and pestilent
   congregation° of vapors. What a piece of work is man!
   How noble in reason, how infinite in faculties, in form
   and moving how express° and admirable, in action
   how like an angel, in apprehention how like a god! The
   beauty of the world, the paragon of animals! And yet,
   to me, what is this quintessance° of dust? Man delights
   me not---no, nor woman neither, though by your
   smiling seem to say so.

Rosencrantz. My lord, there was no such stuff in my
   thoughts.

Brave: splendid. *Fretted*: adorned. *Congregation*: mass.
Express: expressive. *Quintessance*: purest extract.

Hamlet. Why did you laugh then, when I said man
   delights me naught.

Rosencrantz. To think, my lord, if you delight not in man,
   what Lenten entertainment° the players shall receive
   from you.

Players and Polonius enter with a great flourish.

Hamlet. Gentlemen, you are welcome to Elsinore.
   O, old friend, thy face is valanced° since I last saw
   thee. *(To Polonius.)* My lord, will you see the players
   well bestowed°?

Polonius. Come, sirs.

Hamlet. Follow him, friends. We'll hear a play tomorrow.
   *(Hamlet detains one of the players as the others exit
   with Polonius.)* Can you play *The Murder of
   Gonzago*?

Player. Ay, my lord.

Hamlet. We'll have 't tomorrow night. You could, for a
   need, study a speech of some dozen or sixteen lines
   which I could set down and insert in 't, could you not?

Player. Ay, my lord.

Hamlet. Very well. Follow that lord. *(Player exits.)*

Lenten entertainment: simple reception, suitable for lent.   *Valanced*: bearded.
Bestowed: lodged.

Hamlet. O, what a rogue and peasant slave am I!
    Who does me this? It cannot be
    But I am pigeon-livered and lack gall
    To make oppression bitter, or ere this
    I should have fatted all the region kites
    With this slave's offal. Bloody, bawdy, villain!
    O, vengeance!
    Why, what an ass am I! This is most brave,
    That I, the son of a dear father murdered,
    Prompted to my revenge by heaven and hell,
    Must like a whore unpack my heart with words.

He hears the players laughing.

    I have heard that guilty creature sitting at a play
    Have by the very cunning of the scene
    Been struck so to the soul that presently
    They have proclaimed their malefactions;
                    I'll have these players
    Play something like the murder of my father
    Before mine uncle. I'll observe his looks;
    If 'a do blench,
    I'll know my course. The spirit that I have seen
    May be the devil, and the devil hath power
    T' assume a pleasing shape; yea, to damn me.
                    I'll have grounds
    More relative than this. The play's the thing
    Wherein I'll catch the conscience of the King.

He exits.

Act III, Scene 1.

Polonius enters with the king, carrying a book. He looks to make sure they are alone and gestures for Ophelia to join them.

Polonius. Ophelia, walk you here...*(To the king.)*
  Gracious, so please you, we will bestow ourselves.
  (To Ophelia.) Read on this book. *(He hands her the book.)* I hear him coming. Let's withdraw, my lord.

They withdraw. Ophelia is far upstage. Hamlet enters and walks downstage, unaware of Ophelia.

Hamlet. To be, or not to be, that is the question:
  Whether 'tis nobler in the mind to suffer
  The slings° and arrows of outrageous fortune,
  Or to take arms against a sea of troubles
  And by opposing end them. To die, to sleep...
  No more...and by a sleep to say we end
  The heartache and the thousand natural shocks
  That flesh is heir to. 'Tis a consumation
  Devoutly to be wished. To die, to sleep;
  To sleep, perchance to dream. Ay, there's the rub,
  For in that sleep of death what dreams may come,
  When we have shuffled off this mortal coil.
  The undiscovered country from whose bourn°
  No traveler returns, puzzles the will,
  And makes us rather bear those ills we have
  Than fly to others that we know not of?
  Thus conscience does make cowards of us all.

Slings: missiles. *Bourn*: boundary.

Hamlet notices Ophelia, who quickly creates the appearance of reading.

Hamlet. Soft you now, the fair Ophelia.

Ophelia walks toward him.

Ophelia. How does your honor for this many a day?

Hamlet. I humbly thank you; well.

Hamlet notices her book is upside down. He takes it, turns it right side up and hands it back to Ophelia.

Ophelia. My lord, I have remembrances of yours,
    That I have longèd long to redeliver.
    I pray you, now receive them.

She hands him some sort of charm or object.

Hamlet. No, not I. I never gave you aught.

Ophelia. My honored lord, you know right well you did.
    There, my lord.

She hands him the object and this time he takes it.

Hamlet. I did love you once.

Ophelia. Indeed, my lord, you made me believe so.

Hamlet. You should not have believed me. I loved you
   not. Get thee to a nunnery°. Why wouldst thou be a
   breeder of sinners? We are arrant knaves all; believe
   none of us.

Hamlet hears a noise from the direction of Polonius.

Hamlet. Where's your father?

Ophelia. (Awkwardly.) At home, my lord.

Hamlet. Let the doors be shut upon him, that he may play
   the fool nowhere but in 'is own house. Farewell.

Hamlet exits.

Ophelia. O, help him, you sweet heavens!

The king and Polonius enter.

Ophelia. O, woe is me, t' have seen what I have seen.

She exits, running past her father.

King. Some danger, which for to prevent he shall
      with speed to England for the demand of our neglected
      tribute. Haply the seas and countries different
      With variable objects° shall expell
      This something settled matter in his heart.
      Madness in great ones must not unwatched go.

Nunnery: convent or brothel. *Various objects*: different environment to divert
him. *This something...heart*: this problem we are unaware of.

Act III, Scene 2.

Enter Hamlet, Horatio and one player.

Hamlet. Speak the speech, I pray you, as I pronounced it
to you, tripingly on the tongue. But if you mouth it, as
many of our players do, I had as lief° the town crier
spoke my lines. Nor do not saw the air too much with
your hand, thus, but use all gently and beget a
temperance that may give it smoothness. O, it offends
me to the soul to hear a robustious° periwig-pated
fellow tear a passion to tatters, to very rags, to split the
ears of the groundlings°. Pray you, avoid it.

Player. I warrant your honor.

Hamlet.   Then make haste!

Player exits.

Hamlet. Observe my uncle. If his occulted° guilt
    Do not itself unkennel in one speech,
    It is a damnèd ghost° that we have seen,
    And my imaginations are as foul as Vulcan's stithy°

*Great flourish of trumpets and drums. Enter King,
Queen, Ophelia, Polonius, Rosencrantz, Guildenstern,
lords, and guards.*

I had as lief: I would just as soon as.   *Robustious:* violent.   *Periwig-pated:*
wearing a wig.   *Groundling:* spectator that paid the least and stood on the floor
in front of the stage.   *Occulted:* hidden.   *Damnèd ghost:* in league with the
devil.   *Stithy:* a smithy that works with anvils.

King. How fares our cousin°?

Hamlet. Excellent, in faith, of the chameleon's dish°: I eat the air°, promise-crammed.

King. I have nothing with this answer°, Hamlet.

Hamlet crosses to Ophelia, who is sitting on the floor, and sits next to her.

Hamlet. Lady, shall I lie in your lap?

Ophelia. No, my lord.

Hamlet. I mean, my head upon your lap.

Ophelia. Ay, my lord. You are merry, my lord.

Hamlet. Who, I?

Ophelia. Ay, my lord.

Hamlet. O G-d, what should a man do, but be merry? For look you how cheerfully my mother looks, and my father died within two hours.

Ophelia. Nay, 'tis twice two months, my lord.

Cousin: close relative.   *Eat the air:* chameleons were supposed to feed on air. *I have...answer*: I have no idea what you are talking about.

Hamlet. So long? O heavens! Die two months ago, and not forgotten yet? Then there's hope a great man's memory may outlive his life half a year.

Trumpets announce the players entrance. Player who plays Lucianus enters, carrying his mask and presents the prologue.

Player.   For us, and for our tragedy,
                        Here stooping° to your clemency,
                        We beg your hearing patiently.

Hamlet. Is this a prologue, or the posy of a ring°?

Ophelia. 'Tis brief, my lord.

Hamlet. As woman's love.

He exits and enter Player King and Player Queen.

Player King. 'Tis thirty years and Hymen did our hands
Unite communal in most sacred bonds.

Player Queen. So many journeys may the sun and moon
Make us again count o'er ere love be done!

Player King. Faith, I must leave thee, love, and shortly
too; My operant powers° their functions leave to do.

Stooping: bowing.   *Posy of a ring*: short inscription in a ring.   *Operant powers*: vital functions.

Player Queen. In second husband let me be accurst!
   None wed the second but who killed the first.

Player King. I do believe you think what now you speak,
   But what we do determine oft we break
   Purpose is but the slave to memory°.
   This world is not for aye°, nor 'tis not strange
   That even our loves should with our fortunes change.

Player Queen. But here and hence° pursue me lasting
   strife
   If, once a widow, ever I be a wife!

Player King. 'Tis deeply sworn. Sweet, leave me here
   awhile;
   My spirits grow dull, and fain I would beguile
   The tedious day with sleep.

He sleeps and Player Queen exits.

Hamlet. Madam, how like you this play?

Queen. The lady doth protest too much, methinks.

Hamlet. O, but she'll keep her word.

King. What do you call the play?

Hamlet. The Mousetrap. 'Tis a knavish piece of work,
   but what of that? We have free souls, it touches us not.

Purpose is but...memory: we often forget our good intentions.   *Aye*: ever.
Hence: the afterlife.

Enter Lucianus.

Hamlet. This is one Lucianus, nephew to the King.

Ophelia. You are as good as a chorus, my lord.

Hamlet. You shall see anon how the murderer gets the
    love of Gonzago's wife.

*Lucianus pours poison into the Player Kings ear. The
Player Queen enters, mimes her distress, Lucianus
comforts her and it is clear she is now infatuated with
Lucianus.*

Claudius rises and stumbles.

Queen. How fares my lord?

King. Give me some light. Away!

*The King hurries out and all but Hamlet and Horatio
follow.*

Polonius. Lights, lights, lights!

Hamlet. O good Horatio, I'll take the ghost's word for a
    thousand pound. Didst perceive?

Horatio. Very well, my lord.

Hamlet. Upon the talk of poisoning?

Horatio. I did very well note him.

Polonius enters.

Polonius. My lord, the Queen would speak with you, and
     presently.

Hamlet. I will come to my mother by and by.

Polonius. I will say so.

Hamlet. "By and by" is easily said. Leave me, friends.

All but Hamlet exit.

Hamlet. 'Tis now the very witching time° of night,
     When churchyards yawn and hell itself breathes out
     Contagion to this world. Now could I drink hot blood
     And do such bitter business as the day
     Would quake to look on. Soft, now to my mother.
     O heart, lose not thy nature.
     I will speak daggers to her, but use none.

Witching time: time when spells are cast.

Act III, Scene 3.

The King enters and is about to kneel in prayer.
Polonius enters.

Polonius. My lord, he's going to his mother's closet.
    Behind the arras I'll convey myself
    To hear the process. Fare you well, my liege.
    I'll call upon you ere you go to bed
    And tell you what I know.

King. Thanks, dear my lord. *(Polonius exits.)*

King. O, my offense is rank, it smells to heaven;
    It hath the primal eldest curse° upon 't,
    A brother's murder.
    Bow, stubborn knees, and heart with strings of steel,
    Be soft as sinews of the newborn babe!
    All may be well.

As he kneels in prayer Hamlet enters.

Hamlet. Now might I do it pat°, now he is a-praying;
    And now I'll do it. *(He draws his sword.)* And so he
    goes to heaven,
    And so am I revenged. That would be scanned°:
    A villain kills my father, and for that,
    I, his sole son, do this same villain send
    To heaven. Why this is hire and salary, not revenge.

Primal eldest curse: curse of Cain; he murdered his brother, Abel.   *Pat*:
opportunely.   *Scanned*: needs to be looked into.

Hamlet. Up, sword.
> When he is drunk asleep, or in his rage,
> Or in the incestuous pleasure of his bed
> Then trip him, that his heels may kick at heaven,
> And that his soul may be as damned and black
> As hell, whereto he goes...Now to my mother.

Hamlet exits.

King. My words fly up, my thoughts remain below.
> Words without thoughts never to heaven go.

King exits same direction as Hamlet.

Act III, Scene 4.
The Queen's Private Chamber.

Enter the Queen and Polonius.

Polonius. Tell him his pranks have been too broad to bear
    with,
    And that your Grace hath screened and stood between
    Much heat and him. I'll shroud° me even here.
    Pray you, be round° with him.

Hamlet. (Off stage.) Mother, mother!

Hamlet enters.

Hamlet. Now, Mother, what's the matter?

Queen. Hamlet, though hast thy father much offended.

Hamlet. Mother, you have my father much offended.

Queen. Come, come, you answer with an idle° tongue.

Hamlet. Go, go, you question with a wicked tongue.

Queen. Nay, then, I'll set those to you that can speak.

Hamlet. Come, come, and sit you down; you shall not
    budge.

Broad: unrestrained.   *Shroud*: conceal. (dramatic irony in that Polonius is
about to die.)   *Round*: blunt.   *Idle:* foolish.

Queen. What wilt thou do? Thou wilt not murder me?
   Help, ho!

Polonius. (Behind the arras.) What ho! Help!

Hamlet. (Drawing his sword.)
   How now? A rat? Dead for a ducat, dead!

*Hamlet thrusts his sword into the arras. Polonius falls
and dies.*

Queen. O me, what hast thou done?

Hamlet. Nay, I know not. Is it the King?

Hamlet opens the arras.

Queen. O, what a rash and bloody deed is this!

Hamlet. A bloody deed...almost as bad, good Mother,
   As kill a King and marry with his brother.

Queen. As kill a King?

Hamlet.   Ay, lady, it was my word.
   Thou wretched, rash, intruding fool, farewell!
   I took thee for thy better. *(To the Queen.)*
   Leave wringing of your hands. Peace, sit you down,
   And let me wring your heart, for so I shall,
   If it be made of penetrable stuff.

Queen. What have I done, that thou dar'st wag thy tongue
    In noise so rude against me?

Hamlet.   Such an act
    That blurs the grace and blush of modesty,
    Calls virtue hypocrite, makes marriage vows
    As false as dicer's oaths. Heaven's face
    Is thought-sick at the act.

Queen.   Ay me, what act?

Hamlet.

*Opens the charm hanging around her neck and shows
her the two likenesses of King Hamlet and Claudius.*

    Look here upon this picture, and on this,
    The counterfeit presentment of two brothers.
    See what a grace was seated on this brow:
    A combination and a form indeed
    Where every god did seem to set his seal
    To give the world assurance of a man.
    This was your husband. Look you now what follows:
    Here is your husband, like a mildewed ear,
    Blasting his wholesome brother. Have you eyes?
    Could you on this fair mountain leave to feed
    And batten on this moor? Ha, have you eyes?
    What judgement would step from this to this?

Queen. O Hamlet, speak no more!
　　Thou turn'st my eyes into my very soul,
　　And there I see such black and grainèd spots
　　As will not leave their tinct°. O speak to me no more!
　　These words like daggers enter in my ears.
　　No more, sweet Hamlet!

The ghost enters.

Hamlet. Save me, and hover o'er me with your wings,
　　You heavenly guards! What would your gracious
　　figure?

Queen. Alas, he's mad!

Ghost. Do not forget. This visitation
　　Is but to whet thy almost blunted purpose.
　　But look, amazement on thy mother sits.
　　O, step between her and her fighting soul!
　　Speak to her, Hamlet.

Hamlet. (Looking at the ghost.) How is it with you, lady?

Queen. Alas, how is it with you,
　　That you do bend your eyes on vacancy?
　　Whereon do you look?

Hamlet. On him, on him! Look you how pale he glares!

Queen. To whom do you speak this?

Leave their tinct: surrender their color.

Hamlet. Do you see nothing there?

Queen. Nothing at all, yet all that is I see.

Hamlet. Why, look you there, look how it steals away!
    My father, in his habit° as he lived!

Ghost exits.

Queen. This is the very coinage of your brain.

Hamlet. It is not madness that I have uttered.
    Mother, for love of grace, confess yourself to heaven,
    Repent what's past, avoid what is to come,
    And do not spread the compost on the weeds
    To make them ranker.

Queen. O Hamlet, thou hast cleft my heart in twain.

Hamlet. O throw away the worser part of it,
    And live the purer with the other half.
    Good night. But go not to my uncle's bed;
    Assume a virtue, if you have it not.
    And when you are desirous to be blest
    I'll blessing beg of you. *(Points to Polonius.)*
                    For this same lord.
    I do repent; but heaven hath pleased it so.

Queen. What shall I do?

Habit: dress.

46

Hamlet. Do not let the bloat king tempt you to bed,
    Pinch wanton° on your cheek, call you his mouse,
    And let him, for a pair of reechy° kisses,
    Make you to ravel all this matter out
    That I essentially am not in madness,
    But mad in craft°.

Queen. Be thou assured, if words be made of breath,
    And breath of life, I have no life to breathe
    What thou hast said to me.

Hamlet. I must to England. You know that?

Queen.   Alack,
    I had forgot. 'Tis so concluded on.

Hamlet. There's letters sealed, and my two schoolfellows,
    Whom I will trust as I will adders fanged,
    They bear the mandate; they must sweep my way
    And marshall me to knavery°. *(Smiling.)* Let it work°.
    (To Polonius.) This man shall set me packing.
    I'll lug the guts into the neighbor room.
    Come, sir. *(Dragging Polonius.)* Good night, Mother.

Wanton: love pinches.   *Reechy*: dirty, filthy.   *Craft:* cunning.   *Marshall*
me...knavery: lead me to treachery.   *Work*: proceed.

Act IV, Scene 1.

Gertrude. Ah, mine own lord, what have I seen tonight!

King. What, Gertrude? How does Hamlet?

Queen. Mad as the sea and wind when both contend
  Which is the mightier. In his lawless fit,
  He hath killed the unseen good old man.

King.   O heavy deed!
  It hath been so with us, had we been there.
  His liberty is full of threats to all...
  To you yourself, to us, to everyone.
  Alas, how shall this bloody deed be answered?
  The sun no sooner shall the mountains touch
  But we will ship him hence.

Act IV, Scene 2 is cut.
Act IV, Scene 3.

*Enter Rosencrantz, Guildenstern, and Lords in great
commotion.*

King. How now, what hath befallen?

Rosencrantz. Where the dead body is bestowed, my lord,
  We cannot get from him.

King.   But where is he?

Guildenstern. Without, my lord; guarded, to know your
  pleasure.

King. Bring him before us.

Rosencrantz. Ho, bring in the Lord.

Two guards escort Hamlet in.

King. Now, Hamlet, where's Polonius?

Hamlet. At supper.

King.   At supper? Where?

Hamlet. Not where he eats, but where he is eaten. A
    certain convocation of politic° worms are e'en at him.

King. Alas, alas!

Hamlet. A man may fish with the worm that hath eat
    of a king, and eat of the fish that hath fed of that worm.

King. What does thou mean by this?

Hamlet. Nothing but to show you how a king may go a
    progress through the guts of a beggar.

King. Where is Polonius?

Hamlet. In heaven. Send thither to see. If your messenger
    find him not there, seek him in the other place yourself.

Politic: crafty.

Hamlet. But if indeed you find him not within this month, you shall nose him as you go up the stairs into the lobby.

King. (To his guards.) Go seek him there.

Hamlet. He will stay till you come.

King. Hamlet, this deed, for thine especial safety for England.

Hamlet. For England!

King. Ay, Hamlet.

Hamlet. To England! *(To the king.)* Farewell, dear mother.

King. Thy loving father, Hamlet.

Hamlet. My mother. Father and mother is man and wife, man and wife is one flesh, and so, my mother. Come, for England!

Hamlet exits.

King. Away! For everything is sealed and done. *(All exit.)*
And, England, if my love thou hold'st at aught°...
By letters congruing° to that effect,
The present death of Hamlet. Do it, England.

Act IV, Scene 4 is cut.

Aught: at any value.   *Congruing*: agreeing.

Act IV, Scene 5

The Queen enters..

Queen. She speaks much of her father, says she hears
There's tricks in the world, and hems, and beats her
heart...Look, she comes.

Ophelia comes running in, followed by Horatio.

Ophelia. Where is the beauteous majesty of Denmark?

Queen. How now, Ophelia?

Ophelia. (Singing.) "He is dead and gone, lady,
He is dead and gone;
At his head a grass-green turf,
At his heels a stone."

King. How do you, pretty lady?

Ophelia. I hope all will be well. We must be patient,
but I cannot choose but weep to think they would lay
him in the cold ground. My brother shall know of it.
And so I thank you for your good counsel. Come, my
coach! Good night, ladies, good night, sweet ladies,
good night, good night. (*She exits.*)

King. (To Horatio.) Follow her close. Give her good
watch, I pray you.

Horatio exits.

51

King. O Gertrude, Gertrude,
    When sorrows come, they come not single spies,
    But in battalions. First, her father slain;
    Next, your son gone, and he most violent author
    Of his own just remove.

Great deal of noise off stage.

Queen. Alack, what noise is this?

King. Attend!

Laertes is heard off stage.

Laertes. Where is the king?

Laertes comes barging in, followed by two guards.

Laertes. O thou vile king, give me my father!

Queen. Calmly, good Laertes.

King. Let him go, Gertrude. *(To guards.)* Do not fear our
    person. *(The guards exit.)*

Laertes. Where is my father?

King.   Dead.

Queen. But not by him.

Laertes. How came he dead? I'll not be juggled with.
   To hell, allegiance!
   Let come what comes, only I'll be revenged
   Most throughly for my father.

King.   Good Laertes,
   If you desire to know the certainty
   Of your dear father, it 't writ in your revenge
   That you will draw both friend and foe?

Laertes. None but enemies.

King.   Why, now you speak
   like a good child and a true gentleman.
   That I am guiltless of your father's death,
   And am most sensibly in grief for it.

Noise off stage.

Laertes. How now, what noise is that?

*Ophelia skips in, singing, followed by a guard who was
unable to stop her.*

Ophelia.   "They bore him barefaced on the brier,
                        Hey non nonny, nonny, hey nony,
                        And in his grave rained many a tear..."

Laertes. Dear maid, kind sister, sweet Ophelia!
   O heavens, is it possible a young maid's wits
   Should be as mortal as an old man's life?

Ophelia. There's rosemary, that's for remembrance;
pray you, love, remember. And there is pansies; that's
for thoughts.

Laertes. A document in madness, thoughts and
remembrance fitted.

Ophelia. There's's fennel for you, and columbines.
There's rue for you, and here's some for me. You must
wear your rue with a difference. There's a daisy. I
would give you some violets, but they withered all
when my father died. *(She exits, singing.)*
"And will not come again?
And will not come again?
No, no, he is dead.
Go to thy deathbed,
He never will come again.

Laertes. Do you see this, O G-d?

King. Laertes, I must commune with your grief,
Or you deny me my right.

Laertes.   Let this be so.

King. Give us leave.

All exit but the King and Laertes.

King. Where the offense is, let the great ax fall.

Act IV, Scene 6 is cut.

Act IV, Scene 7.

King. Young Hamlet hath slain your noble father.

Laertes.   So tell me
    Why you proceeded not against these feats°
    So crimeful and so capital in nature.

King. O for two special reasons.
    The Queen, his mother, lives almost by his looks.
            The other motive
    Is the great love the general gender° bear him.

Laertes. And so have I a noble father lost.
    But my revenge will come.

King. Laertes, was your father dear to you?

Laertes. Why ask you this?

King. Not that I think you did not love your father.
             What would you undertake
    To show yourself in deed your father's son
    More than in words?

Laertes. To cut his throat in the church.

King. Revenge should have no bounds. But good Laertes,
    We'll put a wager on your heads. He, being remiss,
    Most generous, and free from all contriving,
    Will not peruse the foils, so you may choose

Feats: acts.   *General gender*: general public.

King. A sword unbated°, and in a pass of practice°
  Requite him for your father.

Laertes.   I'll do 't.
  And for that purpose I'll anoint my sword.
  I bought an unction° of a mountbank°
  So mortal that where it draws blood
  No cataplasm° can save the thing from death.

King. When in your motion you are hot and dry...
  As make your bouts more violent to that end...
  And that he calls for drink, I'll have prepared him
  A chalice for the occasion, whereon but sipping,
  If he by chance escape your venomed stuck°,
  Our purpose may hold there *(A cry off stage.)*
  But stay, what noise?

The Queen enters.

Queen. One woe doth tread upon another's heel
  So fast they follow. Your sister's drowned, Laertes.

Laertes. Drowned! O, where?

Queen. There is a willow grows askant° the brook,
  That shows his hoar leaves in the glassy stream;
  There with fantastic garlands did she make
  Of crowflowers, nettles, daisies, and long purples,
  There on the pendent boughs° her crownet weeds

Unbated: having no button on the tip. *Pass of practice:* a deadly thrust.
Unction: ointment. *Mountbank:* quack doctor. *Cataplasm:* poultice.
Stuck: thrust. *Askant:* aslant. *Pendent boughs:* unsupported branches.

[Queen] Clamb'ring to hang, an envious sliver broke,
   When down her weedy trophies and herself
   Fell in the weeping brook. Her clothes spread wide,
   And mermaidlike awhile they bore her up,
   Which time she chanted snatches of old tunes,
   As one incapable of her own distress.
                    But long it could not be
   Till that her garments, heavy with her drink,
   Pulled the poor wretch from her melodious lay
   To muddy death.

Laertes.   Alas, then she is drowned?

Queen. Drowned, drowned.

Laertes.   Adieu, my lord.
   I have a speech of fire that fain would blaze,
   But that this folly douts° it.

He exits.

King.   Let's follow, Gertrude.
   How much I had to do to calm his rage!
   Now fear I this will give it start again;
   Therefore let's follow.

They exit.

Douts: extinguishes.

Act V, Scene 1.

The churchyard.

Enter the Gravedigger with shovel and drink.

Gravedigger. (Singing.) "In youth, when I did love, did love,
> Methought it was very sweet,
> To contract the time for my behove,

Hamlet and Horatio enter.

Gravedigger. (Still singing.) "But age with his stealing steps
> Hath clawed me in his clutch,
> And hath shipped me unto the land,
> As if I had never been such."

Hamlet. Whose grave's this, sirrah°?

Gravedigger. Mine, sir.

Hamlet. I think it be thine, indeed, for thou liest in 't.

Gravedigger. For my part, I do not lie in 't, yet it is mine.

Hamlet. What man dost thou dig it for?

Gravedigger. For no man, sir.

Sirrah: a term of address to inferiors.

Hamlet. What women, then?

Gravedigger. For none, neither.

Hamlet. Who is to be buried in 't?

Gravedigger. One that was a woman, sir, but rest her
soul, she's dead.

Hamlet. How absolute° the knave...How long hast thou
been a grave maker?

Gravedigger. The very day young Hamlet was born...
some thirty years... *(He picks up a skull.)*
Here's a skull now hath lien you in the earth three and
twenty years.

Hamlet. Whose was it?

Gravedigger. A whoresome° mad fellow's it was. This
same skull, sir, was Yorick's skull, the King's jester.

Hamlet. This?

Gravedigger. E'en that.

Hamlet. Let me see. *(He takes the skull.)* Alas, poor
Yorick! I knew him, Horatio, a fellow of infinite jest, or
most excellent fancy. He hath bore me on his back a
thousand times, and how now abhored in my
imagination it is. My gorge rises° at it.

Absolute: precise.   *Whoresome:* vile.   *Gorge rises:* I feel nauseated.

Enter the King, Queen, Laertes, Priest, and Lords.
Hamlet and Horatio conceal themselves as Ophelia's
body is taken to the grave.

Priest. Her obsequies have been as far enlarged
　　As we have warranty°. Her death was doubtful,
　　She should in ground unsanctified been lodged°.
　　Yet here she is allowed her virgin crants°
　　Her maiden strewments, and the bringing home
　　Of bell and burial°.

Laertes. Must there no more be done?

Priest. No more be done.

Laertes.　　　　　　　　Lay her in the earth,
　　And from her fair and unpolluted flesh
　　May violets spring!

Hamlet. (To Horatio.) What, the fair Ophelia?

Queen. I had hoped thou shouldst have been my Hamlet's
　　wife. *(Tossing flowers.)* Sweets to the sweet! Farewell.

Laertes.　　　　　　　　Hold off the earth awhile,
　　Till I have caught her once more in my arms.

Laertes embraces Ophelia.

Warranty: ecclesiastical authority.　*She should...lodged:* she should have been buried in unsanctified ground.　*Crants:* garland.　*Bringing...burial:* laying her body to rest in consecrated grounds, with a tolling bell.

Hamlet. What is he whose grief bears such an emphasis?
   This is I, Hamlet the Dane.

Laertes. (Grabs Hamlet by the throat.) The devil take thy
   soul!

Hamlet. I prithee, take thy fingers from my throat,
   For I have in me something dangerous,
   Which let thy wisdom fear.

King. Pluck them asunder.

Queen.. Hamlet, Hamlet.

Horatio. Good my lord, be quiet.

Horatio manages to separate Hamlet and Laertes.

Hamlet. I loved Ophelia. Forty thousand brothers
   Could not with all their quantity of love
   Make up my sum.
   What is the reason you use me thus?
   I loved you ever...But it is no matter;
   The cat will mew, and dog will have his day.

Hamlet exits.

King. I pray thee, good Horatio, wait upon him.

Horatio follows Hamlet.

King. (To Laertes.) Strengthen your patience in our last
   night's speech;
   We'll put the matter to the present push...
   Good Gertrude, set some watch over your son.

They all exit.

Act V, Scene 2.

Hamlet and Horatio enter.

Hamlet. (Still upset.) Wilt thou hear now how I did
   proceed?

Horatio. I beseech you.

Hamlet.   I sat me down,
   Devised a new commission, wrote it fair.
   Wilt thou know the effect of what I wrote?

Horatio. Ay, good my lord.

Hamlet. An earnest conjuration° from the King,
   As England was his faithful tributary,
   Without debatement further more or less,
   He should those bearers put to sudden death,
   Not shriving time allowed.

Horatio. So Guildenstern and Rosencrantz go to 't°.

Conjuration: entreaty.   *Go to 't*: are dead.

Hamlet. Why, man, they did make love to this
　　employment.
　　Their defeat does by their own insinuation° grow.

Horatio. Why, what a king is this!

Hamlet. He that hath killed my king and whored my
　　mother,
　　Popped in between the election° and my hopes...
　　Is 't not perfect conscience to quit him with this arm?

Horatio. Peace, who comes here?

Osric enters, removing his hat.

Osric. Your lordship is right welcome back to Denmark.

Hamlet. I humbly thank you, sir. *(To Horatio.)* Dost know
　　this waterfly?

Horatio. No, my good lord.

Hamlet. Put your bonnet to his right use; 'tis for the head.

Osric. I thank you, your lordship, it is very hot.

Hamlet. No, 'tis very cold. The wind is northerly.

Osric puts his hat on.

Insinuation: sticking their nose in other's business.
Election: (Danish monarch was elected by a small group of electors.)

Hamlet. But yet methinks it is very sultry and hot for my
   complexion.

Osric. (Removing his hat.) Exceedingly, my lord, it is very
   sultry...My lord, his majesty bade me signify to you
   that he has laid a great wager on your head. The King,
   sir, hath laid that in a dozen passes between yourself
   and Laertes, he shall not exceed you three hits.

Hamlet. Let the swords be brought, the gentleman willing,
   and the King hold his purpose, I will win for him an I
   can; if not, I will gain nothing but my shame and the
   odd hits.

*Sounds of the King, Queen, guards, Lords, etc. about to
enter.*

Osric. The King and Queen are all coming down.

*They enter. The King looks to Osric to know of Hamlet's
decision. Oscric smiles and bows, to indicate the dual is
on.*

King. Come, Hamlet, come and take this hand from me.

The King puts Laertes's hand into Hamlet's.

Hamlet. Give me your pardon, sir. I have done thee wrong.
   What I have done, I here proclaim was madness.

Laertes. I do receive your offered love like love,
   And will not wrong it.

Hamlet.   I embrace it freely,
    And will this brother's° wager frankly play...
    Come, give us the swords.

Guards hand them each a blade.

Hamlet.   Very well, my lord,
    Your Grace has laid the odds on the weaker side.

King. I do not fear it. I have seen you both.
    If Hamlet give the first or second hit,
    The King shall drink to Hamlet's better breath.

Trumpets play.

Hamlet. Come sir.

Laertes. Come, my lord.

They play and Hamlet scores the first hit.

Hamlet. One.

Laertes. No.

Hamlet. Judgement.

Osric.   A hit, a very palpable hit.

Trumpets play.

Brother's: amicably, as between friends.

Laertes. Well, again.

King. (He rises.) Stay, give me drink.

King makes a big show of drinking the wine.

King.   Hamlet, this pearl is thine.

The King places a pearl in the cup.

King. Here's to thy health. *(Hands the cup to Hamlet.)*

Hamlet. I'll play this bout first. Set it by awhile.
   Come. *(They play.)* Another hit, what say you?

Laertes. A touch, a touch, I do confess it.

King.   Our son shall win.

Queen. (Taking the cup.) The Queen carouses° to thy
   fortune, Hamlet.

King. Gertrude, do not drink.

Queen. I will, my lord, I pray you pardon me. *(She
   drinks.)*

King. (Aside.) It is the poisoned cup. It is too late.

Carouses: drinks a toast.

Queen. (Offers cup to Hamlet.) I dare not yet, madam; by
and by.

Laertes. (Aside.) I'll hit him now, yet it is almost against
my conscience.

Hamlet. Come, Laertes, pass with your best violence;
I am afeared you make a wanton of me°.

They play. The fight takes on a very aggressive tone.

Laertes. Have at you now!

*Laertes scratches Hamlet with the poisoned tip. Laertes
is disarmed, they exchange blades and Hamlet wounds
Laertes. The Queen falls.*

Osric.   Look to the Queen there, ho!

Horatio. They bleed on both sides. How is it, my lord?

Hamlet. How does the Queen?

King.   She swoons to see them bleed.

Queen. No, no, the drink, the drink...O my dear Hamlet...
The drink, the drink! I am poisoned. *(She dies.)*

Hamlet. O villainy! Treachery! Seek it out!

You make...of me: hold back and treat me like a spoiled child so I can win.

Laertes falls.

Laertes. It is here, Hamlet. Hamlet, thou art slain.
   No med'cine in the world can do thee good.
   The treacherous instrument is in thy hand,
   Unbated and envenomed. The foul practice
   Hath turned itself on me...Exchange forgiveness with
   me, noble Hamlet. Mine and my father's death come
   not upon thee. The King, the King's to blame. *(He dies.)*

Hamlet. The point envenomed too? Then, venom, to thy
   work!

He stabs the King.

King. O, yet defend me, friends! I am but hurt.

Hamlet forces the King to drink.

Hamlet. Here, thou incestuous, murderous, damnèd Dane.
   Drink off this potion. Follow my mother. *(King dies.)*

Hamlet. (Falls.)   Horatio, I am dead,
   Thou livest. Report me and my cause aright
   To the unsatisfied.

Horatio.   Never believe it.
   I am more an antique Roman° than a Dane.
   Here's yet some liquour left.

Horatio attempts to drink and Hamlet stops him.

Roman: (It was a Roman custom to follow their masters in death.)

Hamlet.   As thou'rt a man,
    Give me the cup! Let go! By heaven, I'll have it.
    If thou didst ever hold me in thy heart,
    Draw thy breath in pain to tell my story...
    O, I die, Horatio!...The rest is silence.

He dies and all is quiet.

Horatio. Good night, sweet Prince,
    And flights of angels sing thee to thy rest!

The end.

Other Fine Titles From
Five Star Publications, Incorporated

Most titles are available through
www.BarnesandNoble.com and www.amazon.com

Shakespeare: To Teach
or Not to Teach
By Cass Foster and Lynn G. Johnson
The answer is a resounding "To Teach!"
There's nothing dull about this guide
for anyone teaching Shakespeare in the
classroom, with activities such as
crossword puzzles, a scavenger hunt,
warm-up games, and costume and
scenery suggestions.
ISBN 1-877749-03-6

The Sixty-Minute
Shakespeare Series
By Cass Foster
Not enough time to tackle the
unabridged versions of the world's
most widely read playwright? Pick up a
copy of *Romeo and Juliet, A Midsummer
Night's Dream, Hamlet, Macbeth, Much
Ado About Nothing* and *Twelfth Night*,
and discover how much more accessi-
ble Shakespeare can be to you and
your students.

Letters of Love:
Stories from the Heart
Edited by Salvatore Caputo
In this warm collection of love letters
and stories, a group of everyday people
shares hopes, dreams and experiences
of love: love won, love lost, and love
found again. Most of all, they share
their belief that love is a blessing that
makes life's challenges worthwhile.
ISBN 1-877749-35-4

Linda F. Radke's Promote Like a
Pro: Small Budget, Big Show
By Linda F. Radke and contributors
In Linda F. Radke's *Promote Like a Pro:
Small Budget, Big Show*, a successful
publisher and a group of insiders offer
self-publishers a step-by-step guide on
how to use the print and broadcast
media, public relations, the Internet,

public speaking and other tools to mar-
ket books—without breaking the bank!
ISBN 1-877749-36-2

The Economical Guide
to Self-Publishing
By Linda F. Radke
This book is a must-have for anyone
who is or wants to be a self-publisher.
It is a valuable step-by-step guide for
producing and promoting your book
effectively, even on a limited budget.
The book is filled with tips on avoiding
common, costly mistakes and provides
resources that can save you lots of
money—not to mention headaches. A
Writer's Digest Book Club selection.
ISBN 1-877749-16-8

That Hungarian's in My Kitchen
By Linda F. Radke
You won't want that Hungarian to leave
after you've tried some of the 125 Hun-
garian-American Kosher recipes that
fill this delightful cookbook. Written for
both the novice cook and the sophisti-
cated chef. It comes complete with
"Aunt Ethel's Helpful Hints."
ISBN 1-877749-28-1

Kosher Kettle: International Adven-
tures in Jewish Cooking
By Sybil Ruth Kaplan,
Foreword by Joan Nathan
With more than 350 recipes from 27
countries, this is one Kosher cookbook
you don't want to be without. It
includes everything from wheat halva
from India to borrekas from Greece.
Five Star Publications is donating a
portion of all sales of *Kosher Kettle* to
MAZON: A Jewish Response to Hunger.
A *Jewish Book Club* selection.
ISBN 1-877749-19-2

Other Fine Titles From
Five Star Publications, Incorporated

Most titles are available through
www.BarnesandNoble.com and www.amazon.com

Household Careers: Nannies, Butlers, Maids & More: The Complete Guide for Finding Household Employment
By Linda F. Radke
There is a wealth of professional positions available in the child-care and home-help fields. This award-winning book provides all the information you need to find and secure a household job. ISBN 1-877749-05-2

Nannies, Maids & More: The Complete Guide for Hiring Household Help
By Linda F. Radke
Anyone who has had to hire household help knows what a nightmare it can be. This book provides a step-by-step guide to hiring—and keeping—household help, complete with sample ads, interview questions, and employment forms. ISBN 0-9619853-2-1

Profits of Death: An Insider Exposes the Death Care Industries
By Darryl J. Roberts
This book still has the funeral and cemetery industries reeling from aftershocks. Industry insider Darryl J. Roberts uncovers how the death care industry manipulates consumers into overspending at the most vulnerable time in their lives. He also tells readers everything they need to know about making final arrangements—including how to save up to 50% in costs. THIS IS ONE BOOK THEY CANT BURY!
ISBN 1-877749-21-4

Shoah: Journey From the Ashes
*By Cantor Leo Fettman
and Paul M. Howey*
Cantor Leo Fettman survived the horrors of Auschwitz while millions of others, including almost his entire family, did not. He worked in the crematorium, was experimented on by Dr. Josef Mengele, and lived through an attempted hanging by the SS. His remarkable tale of survival and subsequent joy is an inspiration for all. *Shoah* includes a historical prologue that chronicles the 2,000 years of anti-Semitism that led to the Holocaust. Cantor Fettman's message is one of love and hope, yet it contains an important warning to new generations to remember—in order to avoid repeating—the evils of the past.
ISBN 0-9679721-0-8

For the Record: A Personal Facts and Document Organizer
By Ricki Sue Pagano
Many people have trouble keeping track of the important documents and details of their lives. Ricki Sue Pagano designed *For the Record* so they could regain control—and peace of mind. This organizing tool helps people keep track and makes it easy to find important documents in a pinch.
ISBN 0-9670226-0-6

Tying the Knot: The Sharp Dresser's Guide to Ties and Handkerchiefs
By Andrew G. Cochran
This handy little guide contains everything you want (or need) to know about neckties, bow ties, pocket squares, and handkerchiefs—from coordinating ties and shirts to tying a variety of knots.
ISBN 0-9630152-6-5

Other Fine Titles From
Five Star Publications, Incorporated

Most titles are available through
www.BarnesandNoble.com and www.amazon.com

Phil Rea's How to Become a Millionaire Selling Remodeling
By Phil Rea
All successful remodelers know how to use tools. Too few, however, know how to use the tools of selling. Phil Rea mastered the art of selling remodeling and made more than $1,000,000 at his craft. He has shared his secrets through coast-to-coast seminars. Now, for the first time, you can read how to make the most of the financial opportunities remodeling has to offer.
ISBN 1-877749-29-x

Joe Boyd's Build It Twice...If You Want a Successful Building Project
By Joe Boyd
In *Joe Boyd's Build It Twice...If You Want a Successful Building Project*, construction expert Joe Boyd shares his 40 years of experience with construction disputes and explains why they arise. He also outlines a strategy that will allow project owners to avoid most construction woes: Build the project on paper first!
ISBN 0-9663620-0-4

Light in the Darkness
By St. George T. Lee
Physician St. George T. Lee's sex addiction cost him his career and nearly his family. In *Light in the Darkness*, Dr. Lee talks openly of his treatment and how he fought to regain the respect of his family. His book will serve as a beacon of inspiration for others affected by addictive behaviors of any kind.
ISBN 0-967891-0-1

Getting Your Shift Together: Making Sense of Organizational Culture *and Change*
By P.J. Bouchard and Lizz Pellett
Few things are inevitable: death, taxes—and change. In today's fast-paced business environment, changes come in staggering succession, yet few corporate change initiatives succeed. *Getting Your Shift Together: Making Sense of Organizational Culture* and Change offers solutions to make change an ally that boosts morale, productivity, and the bottom line.
ISBN 0-9673248-0-7

Keys to the Asylum
By Dr. Daniel K. Bloomfield
Invited to become the dean of a one-year medical school in Urbana-Champaign, Dr. Daniel K. Bloomfield said he would have to decline the offer if there were no plans to make it a full four-year school. "Well, that might happen," the bureaucrats said. On that thin hope, he became enmeshed in a 14-year battle with the system: first, to create an innovative medical curriculum on a low budget, then to expand the school, and then to simply keep it alive. Dr. Bloomfield has recorded his grueling experience in *Keys to the Asylum: a Dean, a Medical School, and Academic Politics*. ISBN 0-9701022-0-8

The Proper Pig's Guide to Mealtime Manners
By L.A. Kowal and Sally Starbuck Stamp
Of course, no one in your family would ever be a pig at mealtime, but perhaps you know another family with that problem. This whimsical guide, complete with its own ceramic pig, gives valuable advice for children and adults alike on how to make mealtimes more fun and mannerly.
ISBN 1-877749-20-6